# Dear Parent:
## Your child's love of reading starts here!

Every child learns to read in a different way and at his or her own speed. Some go back and forth between reading levels and read favorite books again and again. Others read through each level in order. You can help your young reader improve and become more confident by encouraging his or her own interests and abilities. From books your child reads with you to the first books he or she reads alone, there are I Can Read Books for every stage of reading:

**SHARED READING**
Basic language, word repetition, and whimsical illustrations, ideal for sharing with your emergent reader

**BEGINNING READING**
Short sentences, familiar words, and simple concepts for children eager to read on their own

**READING WITH HELP**
Engaging stories, longer sentences, and language play for developing readers

**READING ALONE**
Complex plots, challenging vocabulary, and high-interest topics for the independent reader

I Can Read Books have introduced children to the joy of reading since 1957. Featuring award-winning authors and illustrators and a fabulous cast of beloved characters, I Can Read Books set the standard for beginning readers.

A lifetime of discovery begins with the magical words "I Can Read!"

*Visit www.icanread.com for information*
*on enriching your child's reading experience.*

*To the educators of the world—*
*thank you for shaping our children*
*to be independent thinkers!*
*—K. D. & S. R. J.*

The full-color artwork was created digitally.

I Can Read® and I Can Read Book® are trademarks of HarperCollins Publishers.

Cece Loves Science: Push and Pull. Text copyright © 2020 by Kimberly Derting and Shelli R. Johannes. Illustrations copyright © 2020 by Vashti Harrison. All rights reserved. No part of this book may be used or reproduced in any manner whatsoever without written permission except in the case of brief quotations embodied in critical articles and reviews. Manufactured in China. For information address HarperCollins Children's Books, a division of HarperCollins Publishers, 195 Broadway, New York, NY 10007.
www.icanread.com

Library of Congress Cataloging-in-Publication Data
Names: Derting, Kimberly, author. | Johannes, Shelli R., author.
Title: Cece loves science : push and pull / by Kimberly Derting and Shelli Johannes.
Description: First edition. | New York, NY : Greenwillow Books, an Imprint of HarperCollins Publishers, [2020] | Summary: Cece and her friends conduct experiments. Includes glossary and activities using the forces of push and pull.
Identifiers: LCCN 2019032703 | ISBN 9780062946089 (paperback) | ISBN 9780062946096 (hardcover)
Subjects: CYAC: Science—Experiments—Fiction. | Dogs—Food—Fiction. | Force and energy—Fiction.
Classification: LCC PZ7.D4468 Cdp 2020 | DDC [E]—dc23
    LC record available at https://lccn.loc.gov/2019032703

20 21 22 23 24  SCP  10 9 8 7 6 5 4 3 2 1  ❖  First Edition
Greenwillow Books

# Cece
## LOVES SCIENCE

# Push
# and Pull

By KIMBERLY DERTING
and SHELLI R. JOHANNES
pictures based on the art of VASHTI HARRISON

Greenwillow Books
An Imprint of HarperCollins Publishers

Cece and her friend Isaac walked to school.
Cece pulled her dog, Einstein, in a wagon.
Isaac kicked his soccer ball.

Today was a special day.

Ms. Curie met them by the flagpole.

"Is Einstein ready for science class?"

Ms. Curie asked.

Einstein hopped out of the wagon and barked.

"Woof!"

"Einstein is excited!" said Cece.

Cece was excited, too.

Cece loved science.

She could not wait to get started

on a new experiment.

"Today we will learn about push and pull," said Ms. Curie. "These are forces that move objects in different ways.
Can anyone think of an example?"
Cece raised her hand.
"It's like when I pull Einstein in my wagon," she said.

Isaac raised his hand.

"And when I kick my soccer ball,"
he said.

"Exactly!" said Ms. Curie.

"Now, let's do our lab and see
how these forces work."

"Your mission is to make a treat dispenser for our special guest, Einstein," said Ms. Curie.

"Woof!" barked Einstein.

Cece, Isaac, Sam, and Emily
were on Team 1.
Daisy, Caroline, Jacob, and Zara
were on Team 2.

Ms. Curie gave each team the same materials. "You need to use all of these items to solve the problem," she said.

Each team had scissors, a ruler, tape,
a pencil, a cardboard box, cardboard tubes,
and a paper cup.

They also had a toy dump truck, a marble,
string, dominoes, and some doggie treats.

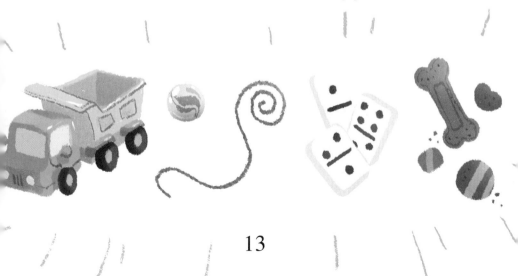

Cece, Isaac, Sam, and Emily
studied the materials.

"What should we do first?" said Isaac.

"I know!" said Cece. "We can build a ramp
for the truck."

"Yes!" said Emily. "And the truck can haul the marble up the ramp."

"This is going to be fun!" said Sam.

"Woof!" barked Einstein.

Sam measured
the cardboard box.

He cut it into
three flat pieces,
one rectangle
and two triangles.

Emily taped
the pieces together.

Cece put the marble in the truck
and pushed the truck up the ramp.

"When you push something,
you are applying force to it," Ms. Curie said.
"In this experiment,
your push is the force
moving the truck up the ramp."

Einstein put his paws on the counter.

He pushed the hamster cage with his nose.

The hamster jumped off his wheel,

landed on his ball, and rolled.

His food bowl tipped over. Splat!

Einstein wagged his tail.

Cece pulled him away from the counter.

"Einstein, Gus doesn't want
to play with you," she said.

"What's next?" asked Emily.

"We can build a tunnel for the marble!" said Cece.

Emily and Sam taped the tubes together to make a tunnel.

Cece flicked the marble
out of the truck.

It rolled down the ramp
and into the tunnel.

The team watched the marble roll
out the other side.
"Excellent!" Ms. Curie said.

Einstein jumped up and put his paws on
the counter again.

He pressed his nose against the fish tank.

The tank slid across the counter.

Water sloshed out. Splash!

"Einstein!" said Cece. "Sit!"

"Maybe we can put a treat in the cup," said Emily.

"So when we push the cup over, the treat falls out," said Isaac.

"That will make him happy!" said Sam.

"How do we use the dominoes?"
asked Emily.

"I think the marble will push over
the dominoes," said Cece. "If it rolls fast
enough."

"And the dominoes will push over the cup,"
said Sam.

The team lined everything up.

"Let's try it," said Cece.

"Woof!" barked Einstein.

Emily rolled the marble
into the first domino.

The first domino hit the second domino
and pushed it over.
The second domino pushed
the third domino over.

When the last domino toppled,

it hit the cup,

and the cup tipped over.

The treat fell.

Einstein gobbled it up.

"It worked!" Isaac said.

"Oh, no!" said Cece.

"What?" asked Emily.

"We forgot to use the string!"
Cece said.

Sam shrugged. "Any ideas?" he said.

Cece picked up the piece of string.

"I wonder if it is strong enough to pull the truck," she said.

"Let's test it," said Emily.

She grabbed the other end of the string

and pulled.

Cece fell to the floor.

Einstein licked her face.

Cece giggled. "I guess pulling can be a super-strong force."

Her team laughed.

"We can tie the string to the truck," said Emily, "and pull the truck up the ramp."

The team set up the experiment again.

Cece pulled the truck up the ramp.

Sam pushed the marble out of the truck.

The marble rolled through the tunnel.

It pushed over the first domino.

The last domino pushed over the cup.

The treat flew
out of the cup.

This time, Einstein caught the treat
and gobbled it up.

"We did it!" said Cece.

"Good job, everyone!" said Ms. Curie,
when both teams had presented
their push-and-pull treat dispensers.

"Woof!" barked Einstein.

"I guess Einstein loves science, too!"
said Isaac.

"And treats," said Cece, hugging Einstein.

Cece loved science,

but she loved Einstein most of all.

# Cece
## LOVES SCIENCE

## Having fun with Push and Pull

### Bowling (PUSH)

Line up some empty plastic water or soda bottles.

Roll a ball across the floor and try to hit a bottle.

What happens if you roll the ball faster?

What happens if you build a ramp for the ball?

What happens if you fill the bottles with water?

Why?

# Tug-of-War (PULL)

Find a thick rope or roll up a piece of fabric (such as a bedsheet).

Tie a ribbon in the middle and mark the center spot on the ground.

Have one person grab each end.

See who can pull the ribbon over to their side.

What happens if you add people to one side? To both sides?

What happens if you all sit down while pulling?

Why?

# Glossary

**Force:** the *push* or *pull* on an object. A force can cause an object to move faster, slow down, remain in place, or change shape.

**Push:** a force that moves something away from you.

**Pull:** a force that moves something toward you.

**Motion:** the change of position of an object because of a force.

Push or pull?

Push or pull?

Push or pull?

Push or pull?